Your official Silicon Valley family of literary journals devoted to the global reader community

FICTION Silicon Valley

Monthly AUG 2016

FICTION Silicon Valley
Monthly AUG 2016

eBook Edition
ISBN-10:1-61978-134-4
ISBN-13:978-1-61978-134-4

Paperback Edition
ISBN-10:1-61978-135-2
ISBN-13:978-1-61978-135-1

From the Editor

Here we are; the first ever issue of FICTION Silicon Valley. I can't believe the day has finally arrived. I am so excited to have the chance to introduce you to some great authors and I hope you find a new favorite among the pages of this literary journal.

I believe that FICTION Silicon Valley will thrive and grow with your support. How can you support FICTION Silicon Valley?

I'm glad you asked.

There are three ways to help FICTION Silicon Valley grow:

#1: If you haven't already, join the FSV Family. It's free and you get *FICTION Silicon Valley Monthly* in eBook for free along with Bonus Bucks toward your purchase of the paperback edition. You can subscribe at FSV's website right here (http://fictionsv.com/index.html).

#2: Tell others about FICTION Silicon Valley. We can only grow if you spread the word. So get out there and tell at least 2 friends we exist and are here to introduce them to some amazing new authors with great prose and poetry.

#3: Become a Patreon Family Member of FSV and get access to even more of what you love from FICTION Silicon Valley. Check out our Patreon page (http://tiny.cc/patreonfsv) for more info about the bonuses and upgrades available to Patreon Family Members.

A Moment in the Rain
by Bethany Gray

I used to love the sound of rain on the roof at night—from the first hesitant tapping to the solid drumming counterpoint to the wind. It was raining hard the night the harp was delivered. I was holed up in the small cottage Ryan and I had rented near Sonoma—that's NorCal wine country, in case you're not familiar. I was waitressing back then for a fancy inn that did a lot with figs and goat cheese.

It must have been a Monday, my day off. I had fallen asleep on the couch when the doorbell woke me. It was early in the evening, and unlike me to nap, but I'd been feeling so tired lately. Ryan wasn't due home for another few days. Still, I went to the door. I peered through the peephole and saw a flash of headlights on the road. I blinked away the afterimage and recognized the package on the front porch. I brought it inside.

I went to get a scissors, then turned back when the sound of wind and rushing rain filled the room. A woman stood next to the package, the door ajar behind her. She was petite—maybe five feet tall at the most, wearing a deep blue cloak like someone from a Renaissance fair.

She was pale with milk white skin, black hair with a widow's peak, and gray eyes like storm clouds.

"Can I help you?" I said, reflexively channeling my waitressing script.

"I came with the harp," she said.

"Oh, you're Irish—I love your accent!"

She nodded.

"I'm Lizzie," I said.

"Roisin."

"Hang on a sec." I got my purse and dug out a ten for a tip. "Thanks for taking the trouble, it's pretty wild out there tonight." I held out the ten, but she didn't take it. Maybe she wanted to warm up for a few minutes. I closed the door and the room grew quiet.

I set about unpacking the portable harp. It was as beautiful as I remembered as it emerged from the bubble wrap. Smooth wood painted green with gilt roses, it looked out of place in the ordinary living room—more fitting for a pub with a fireplace, or a stone cottage someplace where people still put out milk for fairies. But I wanted to hold onto that place, that place where Ryan had proposed. The ring on my finger still felt new.

Ryan had needed to go on a business trip to Dublin— he was in tech, so we'd gone over early for a vacation, and he'd stayed on after I left. We found the harp in a curious little shop in the countryside on one of our day trips. The sound it made reminded me of rain. Ryan bought it for me on the spot and we had it sent home. My heart lifted with happiness at the memory.

"I want to learn to play," I said. I ran my hand along the smooth wood, let my fingers brush against the strings. "Maybe we'll have a harpist at the wedding." I smiled, remembering the warmth of Ryan's laugh. "Do you play?" I asked her.

"No, I was a keener."

"A keener?"

"I used to sing at funerals."

"Wow, that's intense. Is that an Irish thing?"

"Yes. It was sad and uplifting, but now I sing the moment and only for the Irish and their descendants."

"The moment?" I said, thinking that sounded sort of hippy-dippy, but then again she was wearing a cloak.

"The moment of death, for the family of the one who's gone. Or going." She tilted her head, staring at me.

The air seemed charged and heavy, as if lightning were about to strike. I could swear the hairs on the back of my neck stood up. A thought pushed against the back of my mind—a thought about those fairy legends I'd read on vacation.

"You should go now," I said.

"Soon," she said. "You love him very much. I can feel that." She reached out and touched my hand. Her fingers were icy, the chill moving up my arm. I jerked my hand away, but the cold stayed with me.

"No," I said. The air was dense and hard to breathe. She looked at me steadily.

Banshee. The word rose up in my mind, a terrible grief.

"You know me now, and that's a fact," she said.

This woman was impossible—ridiculous, but every cell in my body knew her without question. I fought back with words. "I'm not Irish. And Ryan—he's not my family, not yet—not until the wedding." I stifled a sob.

"True enough." She dropped to her knees, eyes level with my navel. "But it isn't you I came to sing to." She opened her mouth and she sang—a high, keening sound filled with all the wildness of the storm outside and all the sadness in the world. The pain of terrible loss weighed me down like stones piled onto my heart. The room faded and I was there with Ryan, watching helpless through his eyes, his car skidding on the dark, rain-slicked freeway— the oncoming SUV hydroplaning, spinning toward him.

"Lizzie," he said, as glass shattered around him. Then everything went black. I was in the living room with the harp gleaming softly in the lamplight and the sound of the rain on the roof.

About the Author:

Bethany Gray writes stories about things just below the surface of your life that you can almost see out of the corner of your eye. Gray lives in Silicon Valley, where she also writes about passive-aggressive wireless equipment that wants you to think it's your fault. But it's totally not.

Find out more about this artist:

https://www.facebook.com/BethanyGrayAuthor/

Worldshard
by David Colby

Chapter 1: Workshop

There are many shards of many lives. They glint and shimmer in a long string of reincarnations. They are fragmentary. They are incomplete. There are flashes: A man with gray hair, standing before a legate's council, holding up a contract scroll. A woman waving a slogan-poster before a collection of rioters, despite the rocks that whistle past her ear. A teenager with a headband, cradling a crossbow in dream rubble, as enemy soldiers pick their way past the warped and ruined reality that had been her home.

There were more shards, but none floated to the surface while the soul started to contract. The shards moved together, pushing inwards. Where they fused, there was light. The light started off as a mere candle-flame, then grew brighter and brighter. It hurtled past candle to fire to bonfire to arc-light to mana-searcher to artificial sun. Then, when it seemed as though it could get no brighter, the light faded to nothing, leaving only a blurred splotch in the air that faded sluggishly, as if it was unwilling to be forgotten.

With the splotch gone, there was only fog, wreathed around a glittering, perfect, peerless diamond.

Mithril tweezers, held by rubberized gloves which themselves wrapped all too human hands, closed around the diamond and lifted it up.

"Careful." Engineer Lanisbe spoke, his voice muffled by wrappings and a gas mask, eyes bugging out: plastic caps, illuminated from within by tiny etchings along the internal panes. Mana flickered along those etchings, bringing to life shamanistic schematics and theomagical protocol – complexities encoded in a few glyphs here, a few glyphs there, all of them painting a picture of the task to come.

"I'm being careful," Trasik, the engineer holding the tweezers, shot back. He turned away from the focusing point, where the lives had been collapsed into a single soul, and then set the diamond down into a resting cup.

"You can never be too careful," Lanisbe said.

"Give it a rest."

The resting cup glowed, powering up a sustenance field. The diamond floated in the middle of the hazy blue illumination, and in this illumination, it was kept safe from the ravages of time, the distortions of space. The soul within quieted, losing self-awareness, if only for this moment. The two engineers kept their gloves on – those, and their gasmasks, their goggles, their hairnets, their thick faux-leather jackets, their rubber soled boots. All combined to keep human flesh from searing before the crackling flow of mana, the harsh, scouring light of the unfiltered essence of creation.

Crystalline beakers burbled. Liquids flowed through them, burning mana-lights kept them warm – and in one case, boiling hot. Intricate silver and mithril tools were laid out beside a vat of clay – a soft, green-gray clay, distilled from places that even the highest members of the Korvosan bureaucracy didn't know about.

"So, girl or boy?"

"What?" Lanisbe looked at his partner.

Trasik grabbed up huge hunks of clay and slapped them onto the operating table. "Girl or boy?"

"I'm not even going to dignify that question with an answer," Lanisbe said, reaching across the operating table to grab a circle cutter. He frowned, then moved around, so that he could get to the tools easier. Trasik worked quickly. He slapped the clay into shape, creating the outline of a human body, his gloves glowing with guided flares of mana, turning will into reality. Clay formed and molded a thousand times faster than cruder means could manage.

"Come on, we need to strategize here." Trasik carved breasts, hips, a body sculpted less for war and more for…adoration.

"The Autarch wants a front line combatant, by the Dead Gods," Lanisbe said, waiting for his chance to step in. Trasik sighed, then started to slap down more clay.

"Boys aged fourteen to sixteen are showing a marked *lack* of interest in our Champions. And why is this? Because they're a bunch of boring *dudes*, and old ones at that. They've got no sex appeal. Well, Loco does, but that's more for the ladies…"

Lanisbe managed to give his companion a scathing look, despite the gas mask, the head wrappings, the mana-infused goggles. Trasik continued, impervious to the censorious glare.

"Girls can look up to her, but we want boys to be requisitioning her merchandise at the gift dispensaries, having her posters on the wall, yanking their-"

"Stop! Stop…strategizing! For my sanity, if for nothing else." Lanisbe shook his head and used his circle cutter. He sliced into the arm, opening up what could be called muscle if it were not unfeeling clay. He stepped away from the operating table and moved to the conveyor belt that ran alongside the workshop. Already, the conveyor belt was starting to turn, and the fruits of labor were starting to arrive.

Throughout the manufactorum, there were a full three hundred and thirty-three engineering teams. Most of them worked in larger chambers than the cramped, two person operating theater – they worked in vast teams, bent low over conveyor belts, their fingers working a single part here, a single part there. Their parts were moved along, and then fashioned into larger pieces, then those pieces became components of other, larger artifacts. It took the engineering and magical skill of a nation to build a Champion – all of it focused on the finest Glorious Surgeon and the finest Shaper in Imperial Krovsa.

The finished implants, each one the end result of entire factories worth of work, were placed on the final belt.

The belt turned.

And the implants arrived for Lanisbe to pick up and place, solemnly, into the proper mounting points, murmuring under his breath, speaking the prayers that affixed the implants, activating their inherent magical potential. Quickening them.

"Fivefold Muscular Enhancement?"

Trasik, the hardest part of his duty done, picked up a crystal sheaf, unrolling the jade encrusted quipu at the base. He used his finger – still buzzing with the mana he had used to shape the clay – to check one of the listed implants off. The quipu's beads shifted, to show the record was being finalized, then stored in the Sagacious Imperial Bureaucracy Knowledge Vaults.

"Check."

Lanisbe used a scalpel to cut into the clay chest. Six baubles, each one showing an image within: A young man or woman, flying through the air as if a bird or dragon.

"Boundless Wings Dream Form?"

"Check."

The head was opened and opals were placed where the eyes would be.

"Thaumographic Spirit Sight Eyes?"

"Check…Flip her over," Lanisbe said, gesturing. Then he stopped. "Damn it. Damn it, now you have me gendering it. It doesn't even have a soul yet, you…"

Trasik laughed, reaching out and activating the table's mechanism. A grating closed around the clay, holding it into place as the real taxing work began: Blue Jade feathers, hundreds of them, each one hand crafted, started to come down the conveyor belt. They had to be stitched into just the right position along the steel and brass bracings, which themselves had to be bolted into clay shoulder blades.

"Angel Transhuman Implantation…complete. Check."

Lanisbe looked up, even as the last feather settled into place.

"Halfway done." Trasik slapped a clay buttocks. "This has to be the best damn job in the whole of Korvosa."

When the last implant was placed and the final prayers were said, the time came for the most difficult and yet most effortless part of the entire procedure. Trasik picked up the tweezers. Lanisbe took up the containment cup and held it above the head of the clay and brass and steel construct that lay between them. The tweezers glinted, reaching into the sustenance field, grasping onto the diamond. Inside the diamond were the shards of memory: The man, the woman, the child. The hero, the hero, the hero. Reincarnated a dozen times, and a dozen times a different hero, and now, all the potential, all the memories and skills of those past lives were concentrated into a single diamond.

It was the most precious thing in the room and, right now, it was as fragile as a spider web. A single moment of indecision, of lack of focus, could rip the component soul from the diamond, scattering the memories throughout the Sunder and dragging the soul into the Eye – the swirling storm of souls around which the whole of the Sunder turned. Once in the Eye, a heroic soul would have to live another lifetime, and countless man hours of work, ton lots of magical materials, incalculable amounts of magical energy, all of it…would be wasted.

Trasik lowered the tweezers and, his rubber hands shaking slightly with nerves, he released them. The diamond fell.

The diamond landed on the forehead. Clay opened of its own accord and sealed around it. Then the engineers stepped backwards as the workshop's machines came to eager life. Klaxons wailed throughout the entire capitol city, telling all to rush to their living tapestries, to their crystalline projectors. At factories, shifts were ended early. At barracks, recruits and veterans stood side by side, in uniform, their eyes glued to moving images. All across the city – and soon, all across Korvosa…every eye was watching the clay figure.

The machinery grabbed it under the arms and lifted it up, carrying it through a chute in the ceiling to the next room over. This room was surrounded by cold iron with soulcidian backing, preventing any mana from escaping. If a human stepped into the room, it was an even toss as to which killed them first: Mana burn or frostbite. Mana was only liquid in the deepest cold, the cold only found in the deepest Sunder or in hardened labratoria.

The clay body was lowered, inch by inch, into the mana.

Eyes flashed open and the body twitched, writhed. A back arched and characteristics formed: Red hair, short cropped and jagged – like crystals. Blue skin, contrasting with the hair. Green eyes which whirred and clicked, the irises more similar to a memory captor than to a human's eyes.

Wings made of blue jade and steel fluttered reflexively. Arms corded with hissing pistons came to life, flexing muscles of living clay and brass machinery. Toes wiggled. But the sexual characteristics carved by Trasik remained intact.

"We're getting a designation!" Trasik grinned, his eyes bouncing from the view of the vat and the moving tapestry that was hooked to the Champion's nascent thought spiders. "*Vengeful Crystalline Hawk 45C*!"

Lanisbe laughed, whooping loudly, all decorum lost in the delirium of this moment. "Yes!"

And in the vat, *Vengeful Crystalline Hawk 45C* blinked a few times, then asked.

"Uh…are we still at war with Korvosa?"

Chapter 2: We Were Always at War…

I wondered if the bureaucrats who were arguing right outside of my cell knew that I could hear every word they said. I didn't have any secondary perceptive augmentations other than my Thaumographic sight, but I still had *ears*. And, more importantly, I could *use* them. And I could speak their language – that information was infused into my brain, burnt in there when I went from being nothing to being Cee. Well, *Vengeful Crystalline Hawk 45C* if you wanted to use the proper designation.

"We needed a *patriot*. A Champion who would fight and inspire others to fight. Who would work and inspire others to work. Someone marketable, someone we could make action figures out of!"

"T-Technically-"

"Don't technically me on this! We have a SURYAN NATIONAL SITTING IN OUR CAPITOL! A Suryan national with enough firepower in her right arm to level half the city!"

"That's not acc-"

"Don't quote accuracy at me either!"

The voice – most likely a higher ranked member of the Bureaucracy of Korvosa – stormed closer to the cell door.

Part of the door shimmered, becoming translucent to both sides as a pair of gray-white eyes looked inside, at me.

I looked back. I sat on the floor, my knees crossed, my wings folded and collapsed behind me. I could blow the door to bits, but I knew the general tactical and technical and magical disposition of the entire capital. That came from a memory shard – a recent one – of a Korvosan man who had worked himself to death, literally to death, to build up the mana cannon fortifications that ringed the city. And, hell, any Korvosan knew the names of their Champions: *Stern Hand of Industry*, the *Invisible Eye*, the *Ebon Hearted Dragon* and *Unstoppable Destructive Locomotive 566*.

They were also all armed, supported by every single ship in the Imperial Korvosan Skyfleet, the Imperial Korvosan Militat, the Imperial Korvosan Milita Levy, the Imperial Korvosan Behemoth Tank Corps, and the Regulators.

Meanwhile, I was alone, had no armor, and a single mana cannon.

So, I sat, glared at the eyes, and asked: "So, uh, no one has actually answered my question? Are *we* still at war with Korvosa?"

"Well…" The gray-eyed man spoke, his voice pitched to carry through the door. "Yes. Surya is still at war with

Korvosa. Of course, this war is more recent than the one that the engineers say that you are remembering."

I cocked my head, not responding just yet.

"In fact, they say that your core memories are almost two centuries old."

I breathed in, then blew out a slow, tired whistle.

"All right then..." I stood up, my arms stretching above my head, my spine whirring and cracking slightly into position.

Gray-eyes looked like he was frowning; from the way his eyes were furrowing. I let a trickle of mana flow from my internal batteries, activating the Thaumographic enhancements. I could see him in glowing, shimmering light, an aura that showed flecks of green, gold and blue. A prompt, brought to me by a thought-spider that crawled from the inside of my eye to my brain, told me that those colors indicated dominance, aggression and assumed social superiority.

Typical Korvosan.

"So," I said, letting my arms drop. "Who are you going to shoot for this? I figure that's still the general plan: When something goes wrong, find the least connected, least politically astute individual, take them behind a chemical shed, and fire a crossbow bolt through the back of their neck. Right?"

The frown lines got deeper.

"I figure you should kill, er, uh, *fire* whichever thaumaturge and ghost-talker didn't notice this soul was born in Surya. Until then…" I raised up both my hands and lifted my two forefingers, a gesture that came naturally, even if I had no actual idea what it meant until I focused on a memory shard: A young soldier, who had taunted enemy snipers by lifting his hand and showing his fingers like so. "Buzz off."

"We have dealt with that mistake." Gray-eyes didn't sound much angrier, but his aura was spiked with jagged red now. "The question is can we salvage anything from this."

"Well, is Korvosa still a gigantic industrial monster of a nation that sits on seven outlaying islands, strip-mining them and enslaving their population?" I asked, false sweet.

"No."

"Really?"

"Our domain now contains thirteen islands."

I scowled, growing increasingly tempted to test out the mana cannon built into my left arm. "Not helping sway me to the glorious Korvosan cause, buddy."

"It should. It shows that we are winning. Surya has lost five of the wars it has fought against us over the last two hundred years. Each time, it gave up more land and more resources. The other nations haven't fared much better. Our only defeat was against the Four Way Fellowship, and their victories lasted as long as a...well, a Lycanshian's bargain."

I snorted, despite myself. Memories from both Surya and Korvosa, they all remembered that Lycanshians were born swindlers. Which, of course, was why their nation had survived a thousand years of being perched only a stone's throw away from the Eye.

"If you renounce your citizenship to Surya, then we will put you into a Cogwheel with four other newly crafted Champions."

"Splurging, aren't you?"

He paused. "Yes, actually."

"So, let me get this straight...you want me to renounce my allegiance to a land of freedom, democracy, and tolerance, a land which has fought for five centuries to be free and independent from Korvosan aggression..." I said, pacing back and forth. "To fight for a nation that has conquered *six* new islands and probably plans to conquer another dozen if it can get away with it. And, as a flavor topping on the protein blend...you want me to do this while serving with a bunch of other trigger happy imperialist Champions who are, and this is just me hypothesizing here, ordered to shoot to kill if I so much as *blink* in the wrong direction."

I held up my hands, as if trying to turn down an overly generous gift. "Whoa now, don't spoil me here!"

"Are you finished?" Gray Eyes asked.

"I could go on, but yeah, that about sums it up." I crossed my arms across my chest.

Gray Eyes tapped on the door. The image pane shifted, shimmered and turned from a two-way view to a living tapestry, actually showing images from a distant place and possibly even a distant time. The only memories I had of living tapestries were from fuzzy, half-there ones of childhood: But those living tapestries were monochromatic. Watching them had been akin to picking sense out of the buzzing chants of cog-priests, not what I saw before me now: Full color, with fluid, rapid motion.

It looked like the view from a powered glider, cutting through the Sunder that stretched between islands. The view was necessarily short, as powered gliders only had a fifteen-foot-wide reality bubble around them to protect them from the Sunder's shaping influence. The empty bubble around the view was immediately truncated by thick, roiling chaos, pure and unfiltered. It was familiar, across a dozen life times, and yet completely unknown to me. I bit my lip.

The Sunder, the chaos, looked like a red haze of swirling clouds – though, that implied a softness that just was not there. The clouds would sometimes shift into jagged spars of crystal, then melt into almost water-like wavelets. Sometimes, there were half-visible ghosts that flickered in and around the Sunder: The hint of a tree. A slight outline of what might have been a building. The spectral outline of humanoid figures, imprinted into the chaos like the shadows seared into rubble after a mega-Merlin mana bomb going off, moved and then were vanished as the waves/crystals/clouds formed around them.

"Wow…a glider, I'm really impressed." I tried to sound unimpressed. Just watching the writhing, burbling froth of chaotic possibility that was the Sunder, especially brought to life with such eerie clarity, was almost hypnotic.

Hypnotic and *creepy*.

"Keep watching."

The glider continued to cut smoothly through the Sunder. It looked like it was approaching an island or a floating city: Another place where reality engines or human prayer and imagination kept the chaos at bay. Then it struck a hard demarcation line, bursting from chaos to order. It started to tumble and I realized something was very wrong, very very wrong. The view didn't show any of the things I expected: No landscape, no city. No reality engines, no people. Just blackness, dotted with shimmering flecks of white light...until a sphere filled the view. It whipped past before I could even register what it was.

The glider shuddered, righting its tumble.

The sphere came into view.

It looked like a big purple marble, the purple broken by cracks of sheer blackness. Other, smaller marbles floated around it. One of them was blue-green, with wispy white...were those clouds? They were clouds. There were other marbles, but I couldn't look at them, I was too busy looking at those clouds.

"What is this?" I whispered. The living tapestry stilled, letting me examine the image at my leisure.

"You know what it is."

I gulped. My throat felt tight and my wings tingled. Mana coursed excitedly through my body. Pistons hissed and clicked. I clenched and unclenched my fists and something that transcended national pride awoke inside me. In every soul – every human soul – there the memories...the memories of a time before the Endwar, before the world turned into the Sunder, before...before all of this. And my soul was no different.

"A Worldshard," I spoke the words, slowly, carefully…as if the universe might strike me down for uttering such a thing without proper reverence. "You found a Worldshard?"

"We found a Worldshard," Gray Eyes' eyes appeared once more on the window, the image banished. "We commissioned the Cogwheel in secret: Five Champions, each one made to face any of the dangers, any of the threats that a Worldshard might bring. You were to be the fire and the tenacity of the Cogwheel."

I closed my eyes.

"I won't lie," his voice was soft. "Unlocking the shard will bring great wealth to Korvosa. But it will also bring wealth to the other nations, albeit in a lesser way, through trade. And with more wealth, the reasons for war dim, giving us all a chance for peace…at least for a short while, no?"

I frowned.

My foot, bare clay, tapped on the floor of my cell.

"I have one request, Autarch."

He didn't seem surprised that I had guessed his position. Of course, anyone else wouldn't have access to the information he had given me…and no one else would have had the authority to show it, even if they did know it.

"And that is?"

"Once this is done and we're all famous and rolling in permanent wealth, let me emigrate to Surya."

"Your memories are two hundred years old-"

"I don't care," I shot back. "You will let me emigrate."

His eyes glinted. "45C, when the Worldshard is in our hands, we'll do better than that: We'll kick you out so hard your wings will fall off."

"Good enough. So, open the door. I want to shake the hand of the…my boss."

There was a longish pause. I saw another figure with a nervous, jittery gray aura come up to the door. The whispered conversation between him and the Autarch – well, it was entirely one sided, the Autarch saying nothing…well, I got the feeling that he was trying to tell Gray Eyes to not even try to get in the same room as me. The door hissed open and the terrified adjutant leaped backwards as Gray Eyes looked at me, face to face, for the first time.

And I froze.

I recognized him. Not his voice – his voice, I had never heard.

But his face.

His face, older and more wizened for sure, was the face of Thrax. Gunner Thrax. Two conflicting titles came to mind: Thrax the traitor, the man who had turned over fifteen automatic crossbow divisions to Korvosa. And the other was Thrax the Hero, the man who had ended a brutal flanking attack against Korvosan forces. I rubbed my temple with one of my fingers and frowned at Thrax.

"I'm his grandson," he explained.

"The resemblance is vomit inducing."

He gestured. I thought he wanted me to follow him. I stepped forward and the walls opened up. Machinery glittered and two spring loaded launchers shot gleaming steel rings. They snapped around my wrists and glowing beams of energy snapped together to prevent my hands from moving. Machinery clicked and clattered, more launchers firing out rings that snapped my wings and ankles and knees together. Before I could fall over, a flat platform rose behind me, attached itself to my back and then started to move out of the room. A gag closed around my mouth, mana sparking and numbing my throat.

And I didn't even *have* vocal implants – but I figured that this kind of thing wasn't custom made for every Champion. They needed to put in the gag for any Champion that might be persuasive enough to just talk their way out of being strapped down.

"For my protection," Thrax's grandson said. "Oh, and before you ask…my name is Autarch Kennx."

"Charmed," I said.

It came out sounding like this: *Arrmned.*

Honestly, I preferred the way I had gotten to the cell: A jolt to the mana batteries while I was hooked into the vats. It was less...uncomfortable to just be unconscious for a bit.

The wheels of the restraining device squealed slightly as Kennx led me through the corridor. The walls were made of solid, writhing, fully possessed soulcidian. That meant it was a prison, a prison designed to hold the people who were going to be executed and the people who *had* been executed. My eyes flicked from left to right, looking at the walls: Faces and hands pressed against the surfaces, as if they were trying to escape. I shuddered as we wheeled past doors that held the prisoners who were waiting for sentence to be passed. I wondered how many of them were actually going to be given the short drop and long stay in the soulcidian and how many would be let out with nothing worse than a few nightmares about wailing voices and begging faces.

At the end of the corridor we came to an elevator, which rumbled straight down. When the door opened, we came to a corridor made of steel and false-wood, one that someone could walk down without getting nightmares. From there, Kennx took me to an office: austere and quiet, without much ornamentation save for a living tapestry that was showing a young woman with blue hair, who was speaking hastily. The sound crystals were muted, but I could catch a few glimpses of meaning from her lips. She was talking about some troop movements in the eastern islands. Behind her, I could see several massive sky barges, their reality fields shimmering faintly even in dry dock, their crews milling on them like ants on an anthill doused in sugar.

My eyes tracked back to Kennx. He slid his hand along a steel desk that rose out of the ground at his presence. He tapped a gemstone button on the desk. A panel slid back and revealed an ink quill sitting in an inkwell, with a contract printed on quality paper, painted with elegant calligraphy and simplified glyphs. The restraints on me relaxed, somewhat, letting my hands move and my mouth open.

"This is a contract." Kennx held it up, waving it in front of my face. "It states-"

"That I submit to any state mandated training, agree to cooperate with your social engineers, and give up my rights to any profits made from my...action figures. Seriously?" I looked at him.

"Your core memories are from a two-hundred-year-old Suryan terrorist," Kennx frowned. "Modern Champions have action figures, moving tapestries, etheric plays, comic books. They have to. Most Champions, those that are loyal and not Suryan terrorists, get 20% of the revenue from these things."

"And the rest pays for vortex arrows to drop on villages that don't pay their taxes?"

"Exactly." He frowned at me.

"Wonderful. Why don't you skip the action figures and just let me do my job?"

"This." He waggled the contract at me. "*Is* your job, 45C. Sign the damn contract or you can emigrate to Surya as scrap metal."

"Fine. I'll sign. Now, will I have to use my eye lasers, or…?"

He handed me the contract and the quill. I read the contract again, just to make sure I hadn't missed anything. One of the memories in my mind was of a humble legalite, who had fought to make sure that citizens – be they Populat, Bureaucrat, Autarch or Hierophant, get their due. That guided me, informed me…enlightened me. The emigration clause was in there. But it had a lot of hefty restrictions, one of which sprang to my lips.

"I have to *salvage* the Worldshard?"

"Well, yes, it is why we created you. It's why we

created four other Champions –at no small expense mind you – to salvage the Worldshard."

"What happens if we fail and have to fall back?"

Kennx looked at me. And he kept looking, slowly cocking an eyebrow.

"…let me sign the damn contract."

I scribbled my designation in two glyphs and two numerals, then looked at him.

"Done."

The restraints popped off my wrists and legs and then rolled away. I flared my wings, stretching slightly. Then Kennx gestured to the windows, which slipped open, revealing a balcony that looked out over the capitol of Korvosa. Wind blew into the room, ruffling my hair and my wings.

"That contract binds you, remember that."

"I know how contracts work." I tapped my forehead. "I have the memories of a *legalite* in here."

He shook his head and gestured to the balcony of the office, saying, "The Champions usually stay in the Aerie. It's the-"

"Big tower at the edge of the city, I know."

"Your social engineers will be waiting there for you. Cooperate with them, and we won't have any problems." He tapped the contract, tapped my designation glyph on it. Names had power, and designations had double that, for they weren't given names. They were chosen, formed out of the memories and thoughts of the soul that lived inside my head, the soul whose memories formed to create my personality and my future. So...

The only reason I had signed was because I knew, distinctly, what it was like to die. Memory shards became fragmentary and confused around death, but the pain was clear enough. But then pain – and memory – was blown away as I stepped up to the edge of the balcony. The wind that rushed around the prison was intense, and warm: heated by the foundries that dotted the capitol of Korvosa. It was a strange thing to see.

Foundries. Tenement blocks. Mana Generators. Reality Field Projection Domes. Agricultural towers. Prisons, like this one, rising out of the rest of the place like black fingers grabbing for the Sunder-filled sky. The city was a marvel of industry and orthodoxy and...I had to be impressed. A man alone can last a day in the Sunder. A faithless but well trained man alone can last a week. A man with faith can last for months. But many men, all with a single idea about the world around them, working in the same factories, for the same future, they can last millennia. As I flew overhead, I could practically feel the people looking up and pointing.

Look there, they would say.

A Champion.

The Aerie in reality and the Aerie in my memories were in conflict.

Most of those memories looked up to see the Aerie where it was because it was always there and it would always be there, a comforting constant in the Sunder, a reminder of their Champions and so on and so forth. But the memories that formed my core – the one that bubbled to the surface of my mind right now – those memories had seen the building from the distance, when Korvosa had first invaded Surya by drawing its mainland alongside the Suryan coastline. From this tower had flown the powered gliders, the war kites, the sky ships and the Champions. They had met Surya's comparatively pitiful militia and slaughtered them within moments. The image was seared into my mind: A distant tower, surrounded by crisscrossed searing beams of blue-white mana, arcing vortex arrows, and other, worse things.

I started to loop around to the Aerie from an oblique angle. I took a moment to look at it with fresh eyes: First with my normal senses, then with my Thaumagraphic overlay. With those, I saw the flowing mana lines that arced into the tower from nearby buildings. The tinting of the mana gave some clues to its purpose: Blue-white for pure energy, which wormed its way through the building like blood vessels (I knew too well how *those* looked, both on the operating table and the battlefield) with the mana transformers working to turn it to hot and cold air, to crystal pure water, to solidified quintessence and to the dispensaries which could produce anything one needed for their day to day living.

I snapped back to standard vision as I came in for the landing. There were several pads that were marked with the glyph for a Champion, and I settled on the one with three people who were waving excitedly at me – even from a distance, their auras had been flashing gold. Landing was fun: I zoomed straight at it, then pumped mana into my wings at the last second, bringing myself to a skidding stop before the waving people, my heels digging two thin furrows in the steel floor of the pad.

Up close, they were clearly engineers but also clearly...not. They wore the traditional gas masks and the gloves, but their clothes weren't suited for the workshop or foundry. The female leader wore high heeled shoes that looked positively dangerous, with a corset and a frilly dress that looked like it had been designed by someone whose only experience with a factory floor was watching someone perform their duties in pantomime in an empty room: It had straps to hang tools from, but they looked more decorative than anything else and there were trailing ribbons that looked like they had been designed to get caught in as many gears as possible. The men that flanked her – subordinates, from their stance and looks – wore similar things, including the high heels and the gloves and the decorative straps. Though they didn't have corsets.

They had codpieces.

With frilly edges, and embroidery.

It was frankly, the most absurd thing I had ever seen, especially with wind blowing their long, braided hair around and the way that the gas masks looked with eyeliner and…and…

I doubled over, laughing. I wiped glowing tears from my eyes, opened my mouth to try and apologize, then saw how cross they were looking. I doubled over laughing again, almost falling to my side, my wings fluttering and chiming in the wind.

"No! No!" I held up one hand. "I…I'll be okay, just…" I snickered. "Give me a second."

"Are you finished?" the woman asked, grabbing her gas mask and tugging it off.

I grinned. "Maybe."

She frowned at me. "Well, you better get used to how we look, Champion. I'm Kessa, this is Vornix and this is Lenard."

"Hello!" Lenard smiled at me.

"We are your social engineers." Kessa hooked her gas mask to her belt and then put her hands on her hips, thrusting her chest out proudly. "We might not work with mithril and steel, but our tools are no less complex or precise than those that put you together. This is our uniform, shaped by a century of dignified practice and careful selection based off ancient Korvosan styles and fashions. So, you better pay attention and listen to us. Or else."

She actually sounded like she had a bit of steel in her. I wiped my eyes off again, my smile fading. "Or else...what?"

"Or else you don't draw the adoration of the right demographics. Or else you don't do your *job* as an icon of Korvosan values. That takes us all one step closer to falling into the Sunder, and I take that sort of thing *very* seriously...so while you might think it's all faff and nonsense, it is *not*. Understand?"

I nodded, my smile completely gone now.

"Understood," I said

"Very good." She gestured to the doorway that led into the Aerie itself. "Now, come. We have to discuss things and we might as well do it out of the wind."

I followed her, Vornix, and Lenard into the building

proper. The walls here were made of steel and were engraved with stylized murals of former Champions, their glyphs worked into the art so seamlessly that their names seemed to shine naturally from their actions: Cutting Justice pushing back a brace of fairies with his bare hands. Invisible Hand of Peace standing between a convoy of Korvosan nomads – almost a thousand years ago – with a single beam sword, lopping off tentacle after tentacle from a Nameless.

These were heroes whose names I should remember with reverence. And part of me did…and that part was glad that none of the murals, so far, seemed to be dedicated to Champions who had made names for themselves as generals or conquerors. No one deserved to be taken by a Changeling or unmade by a Nameless, not even a Korvosan.

"Now," Vornix spoke up, walking to my left, just in front of one of my wings. Lenard was trying his best to not get his face in my crystalline feathers, so I retracted my wings as much as I could in the corridor. "Do you have any talents?"

"Uh…"

"You know, singing, dancing, art, strategy games, etheric sports, physical sports, Sunder sports-"

"Does knowing how to make an IED out of gossamer

and dreams of vengeance count?"

"…no."

I shrugged. "Well, I'm plum out of ideas."

The corridor opened up into a circular hangar bay. Powered gliders and war kites were there, being refitted and repaired and refueled. Modern gliders were incredible looking. Fast, lean and armed with more mana weapons than I had imagined, including crystalline darts that looked like nothing I had ever seen. Lenard and Vornix stepped between me and the view, both frowning, as Kessa used a pen sized mana light to flash across my body. I watched, bemused, as the light shone through the simple shirt and pants that the prison guards had given me.

"Be serious, here." Vornix said. "Every Champion has their fan clubs."

"Fanzines, centerfolds, posters-" Lenard started ticking the options off on his fingers.

"Interviews! They're going to ask you questions about your personal life."

"pornography…lots of pornography…"

"I'm two days old! I don't have a personal life," I said, working hard to ignore Lenard's thousand-yard stare. Kessa knelt down and started to shine her light over my feet. I blinked down at her. "I'm just here to-"

My tongue practically turned itself inside out and my throat seized up. It wasn't as terrible as it could have been – my memories flashed, worried that I was going to strangle, but my body wasn't the squishy flesh of a human: Clay didn't need to breathe, even if it felt as though it were alive sometimes. So, I just relaxed, and remembered the contract. Stupid, stupid. It had stipulated I couldn't talk about the Worldshard…and I had signed it with my designation, my true name.

I could practically hear a half-forgotten legalite professor, teaching my past life about the effects of contracts: *Why, Jimmy boy, all humanity has left is their good name. Reality is gone, the world is gone, all that remains is faith and when faith is codified into words and signed with a true name, then…is it any wonder contracts have such a physical effect? Is it any wonder they are what we build our civilizations on? Is it any wonder the contract between government and governed, between soldier and commander, between tradesman and tradesman, are the glue of all reality?*

My social engineers didn't seem to have noticed my throat tightening, continuing blithely.

"You're just here to be a Champion. So, can you sing?" Vornix sang a few notes of the Korvosan national anthem, joined in by Lenard, then Kessa. In a few moments, they were belting the whole thing out. I coughed, and then tried to sing with them. My voice cracked and hit a resonance with their voices that almost made me worry one of the vortex arrows mounted on the war kites below were going to set themselves off in protest. I winced and shut up, the three social engineers sighing.

"Dance?" Kessa suggested.

"I can punch through two inches of steel," I said, flexing one of my arms, causing the pistons within to whirr, steam to escape one of the joints. "Do you *really* want me to try dancing here?"

"Good point," Kessa frowned, scanning my arm with her pen. "Maybe you'll make a good actor…"

"I doubt it," Lenard muttered. "We can always fall back on ghostwriting."

"I can do that!" Vornix grinned. "I love to stretch the old quill muscles."

"Wait, ghosts write now?" I asked, frowning slightly. "That sounds even worse than keeping them in prison."

"Oh, no, it's just a term!" Vornix explained. "You dictate past life memories to me, or missions that you go on and I'll spice them up. We claim you wrote them, publish them in cheap mana-print books, and we'll instantly spike literacy rates."

Palm. Meet face.

"Hmm, no." Kessa shook her head, gesturing for us to move out. We started to walk, with Vornix and Lenard staying between me and seeing the weapons that were arrayed below. I kept trying to sneak peeks, even as Kessa explained. "The novel idea is so last decade. Modern teenagers enjoy illustrations."

"Comic books!" Lenard snapped his fingers.

"Brilliant!" Vornix laughed. "We can even use simplified glyphics, maybe add in some sex appeal, eh?" He grinned at me, elbowing me in the side.

I looked at him, then looked at myself: Clay, metal, and a cotton tee-shirt.

Sex appeal?

"Love triangle?" Vornix asked.

"Definitely. Make one of them a Populat boy. We'll have to pick one from the right candidates. The other should be someone dangerous." Kessa nodded as we entered into an elevator. She pushed a glyph that looked like a simplified version of the symbol for a Champion.

"Another Champion?" Lenard asked. "Maybe one in her own Cogwheel."

"Obviously," Kessa grinned. "Maybe we can risk introducing the Suryan element."

"If by element you mean my entire personality?" I

asked, cocking an eyebrow.

"Yes, that," Kessa said, waving her hand. "It'll give our Korvosan boys and girls something to feel proud about: We're so irresistible that even a reincarnated Suryan terrorist can't stay away! We can have them on the edge of their seats."

"Well, it is hard to resist mana cannons being aimed at your head," I said, smiling brightly. Inside I was wondering if maybe there was still time to take the "be scrapped for spare parts" option on my contact.

The elevator opened on a carpeted corridor. There were no murals here. The walls were plain, unadorned. The floor, carpeted and comfortable. And standing amidst it all, talking to two mortal workers, was another Champion. He was about eight feet tall and sculpted like a walking god, without much obvious adornments or external implants, wearing only a work-kilt and sandals. But then he smiled and his entire body seemed to light up and get cast in shadow all at once: The planes and features of his hewn form moved as if he were a walking slogan-poster. I half expected glyphs to appear under him: THE AUTARCH WANTS YOU! Or something inane like that. But…

But in person, it was impossible to not hear the anthem in your ears, to hear the drums of war and the desire to go off and fight the good fight Over There in the trenches and the Sunder, to load vortex arrows on sky ships and pilot daring war kites over foreign skies. The urge flared inside of me, his appearance reaching in and grabbing at my soul – the most human part of me. The two mortal workers nodded and hurried off, leaving the Champion free to look over and notice me. He beamed, holding out his hand to me.

"Cee!" He boomed, as if he knew me. His voice was unnaturally deep, but that just made it more impressive. "So pleased to meet you! I'm the *Stern Hand of Industry*, but you can call me Stern."

"P-P-Pleased," I said, taking his hand, gingerly. He shook mine.

"I should leave you to your social engineers. Listen to them. They can make even a lug like me look good." He grinned at me, like I was his best friend in the world. My knees felt like rubber instead of just clay. He walked past me, to the elevator, adjusting his kilt with one hand. The elevator door closed with a ding and I saw that my social engineers all looked a bit misty eyed and impressed, their eyes lingering on the doorway.

I shook my head, trying to remember that "Stern" was a symbol of Korvosan oppression through and through. Even if he was handsome and charming and knew to call me Cee right off the bat and walked like a living god and-

I shook my head again. Kessa coughed.

"So, that was *Stern Hand of Industry*. He is the eldest Champion in the city, almost seven hundred years old. The last of his Cogwheel still alive...he trains the new Champions, between his duties as guardian of the capitol and vanguard of our First Fleet."

I nodded. "So, uh, we get to learn from him?" Maybe this won't be so bad after all.

"Well, when he is free!" Kessa gestured me down the corridor. I saw that it branched off in two directions: One doorway led into what looked like a reading chamber, complete with a moving tapestry that was currently showing two Champions standing before a pool, both male. They held each other in their arms, their gleaming eyes unwavering as they looked at one another. The taller one spoke, then the tapestry formed the glyphs.

I CANNOT BEAR TO BE APART FROM YOU

The tapestry showed the other champion looking aside. He spoke his words with such passion that I drew my hand to my throat, waiting with bated breath.

I CANNOT BEAR IT EITHER...BUT THE FRONT WAITS. THE FIRST FLEET WAITS...

It returned to a view of them and they clung to one another, before the tapestry melted into a glyph that indicated that the images would return after a few short messages from the State. It moved onto a series of glyphic announcements about labor shortages and various other things I didn't give a damn about. Kessa grinned.

"Thinking about becoming an actress now?"

"What? No! Not unless I get to punch things." I scowled at her. Stern and the tapestry and the fact that this carpeted floor felt better than anything I had remembered in any of my memories – it was like walking on clouds! – were making me forget, slightly, the indignation and anger I was supposed to feel.

"We can arrange that. It's not all romance, there's plenty of action plays. Heck, we usually send a tapestry maker out to the major action sites to make sure everyone has a copy of your fights, that always puts asses in seats." Kessa frowned. "Still, we have to get you fitted."

"For my armor?"

"Well, yes, but also for your uniform. I think we can really capitalize on these wings." She sighed. "Those are works of art, through and through."

She gestured me on. "Come along."

Fortunately for my sanity, we weren't taken to a room full of corsets and froofy dresses and other such faff. It seemed that that kind of thing required work, even with mana looms and the measurements that Kessa had taken with her little light device, work that wasn't finished in the time it took me to walk to the fitting room. So, instead, I was shunted to the side, into a room that smelled comforting, familiar.

It smelled like iron and black powder and mana crystals. It smelled like machine oil and lubrication. It smelled like an armory. Along the walls were breastplates, with shoulder guards, protective gloves, greaves, gorgets, bevors, brigandines, hauberks, cuirasses, culets, cowters, spaulders, and schynbalds. And, of course, the machinery that would wed the pieces together, connect them to my insets and then the mana batteries that would power them, adding to my already impressive strength. Then on the other wall were stacks of crystalline cylinders – beam swords – curved bows made out of solid cold iron, miniature vortex arrows, man-portable mana cannons and...

"Oooooooooh..."

I stepped away from Kessa and to what looked like a portable mana cannon...but rather than being mounted on the shoulder, it was held by a brace that extended to the fore of its boxy center. The barrel wasn't a single tube, but rather six slender barrels that looked as though they could rotate. I put my hands on it, before a voice barked – sharp, quick – "Don't even think about touching that, missy!"

I started and spun around to face the man who had barked: an older man, half his face turned into what looked like a moldy fungus, his flesh collapsing inward and replaced by blooms and caps and spores. I tried to not stare as my Thaumagraphic vision showed that half his aura was warbly and twisted. He had been kissed by the Sunder. That was something I never needed to worry about: As a machine, the Sunder couldn't warp my flesh or corrode my sanity. This man had to have been in the military, or in one of the border towns that got very unlucky.

"I do like that you tried to grab it, though." He grinned, a truly grotesque thing to see. "Means that your soul has the right idea."

"Well, name me a single Champion who doesn't have at least one soldier in their past lives." I tried to smile back.

He smirked, also horrifying, and introduced himself. "I'm Sken Half Face, but you can call me Master Armorer. Now, get that shirt off and extend your insets."

I dropped my shirt to the ground, then pushed my pants aside – noting that my social engineers had left, practically fleeing from the scene. It was almost as though they didn't want to be near a horrifyingly disfigured man.

Fancy that.

I focused and my insets extended outwards. They were a series of tiny screws that were mounted at my various joints, the backs of my knees, my thighs, shoulder blades, hips, and so on. The master armorer frowned and looked at them, clucking his tongue.

"Idiots."

"Hmm?"

"They built the insets to suit heavy armor, but your wings are clearly the hallmarks of a mobile fighter. I'm going to check with the design committee about this."

"I can take it," I said, my brow furrowing. In the back of my mind, the words 'sex appeal' floated, obscurely. I ignored it and the strange feeling that I should still be wearing clothes.

The master armorer looked into my eyes, frowning. "If you fall in the Sunder, you fall for a *long* time."

"Yes, I plan to immediately fly into the Sunder without any testing or training whatsoever. Master Armorer, you really see straight through my schemes! Was this a special skill you learned?"

He waggled a finger at me. Thankfully, it was not covered with spores. I still had to repress a flinch, reminding myself that I was immune to the kiss of the

Sunder, and even if I wasn't, he clearly wasn't contagious, or he wouldn't be *working* here.

"Don't sass me. But, well, step onto the platform."

He gestured me forward and I stepped up onto a raised platform that sat in the middle of the room. Once there, I lifted my arms up to make myself into a T, as he picked up a piece of armor and put it to my back, brushing my feathers up so that he could slip it on under my wings. He harrumphed and then locked it into my insets. I closed my eyes and focused. The insets whirred and clicked into place and the armor felt as light as a piece of paper. I grinned.

"Layer it on."

"What?"

"Give me the thickest steel you can put on me while keeping it, you know, articulated."

He harrumphed and started to place pieces. Each one whirred into place and went from heavy to not heavy at all. Once he was done, I flexed my arms, the steel clicking and squeaking softly. Steam hissed from my joints and vents and I grinned, turning to face him, flaring my wings as he looked me up and down, pursing his lips. He tapped a few places in the armor.

"Even a fairie's thinnest blade'd have a hard time finding a soft spot in that. I guess they've improved the insets and, guess what, no one *told* me. Bugger engineers with a wrench."

I snickered. "Can you do that to the socials too? They're driving me crazy."

"We're glad to be appreciated," Kessa said from the doorway of the armory, walking inside.

"We've decided to go for a green, red and blue motif for you," she said, beaming at me. "So, this armor should work once we've repainted it, maybe thought of a logo for you."

I scowled at her. "Couldn't you have at least waited for me to *try* the weapons."

"Oh! Yes! The weapons. They need to be something cool, but also collectable. Something that the children with your action figures can play with and exchange for other sets of equipment..."

"I was once a child," I said, as the master armorer went to rummage in the weapon pile. I glanced at the six barreled mana cannon, but was disappointed, the master armorer didn't go near it. "I was once many children, actually," I added. "I know what kids like. They like any kinds of weapons. You know, so you can take the figure and make pew, kabloosh, foosh, boom, ratta-tata, kplang noises. That hasn't changed, right?"

"...no, it hasn't."

"Then let's pick weapons based off their ability to kill fairies first and treat everything else as secondary." I grinned at her.

She nodded. "Point, taken."

"Wow…you *do* have ears."

She frowned. "Don't push it, Champion."

The master armorer turned back, holding up a dull, circular shield that looked well used, slightly dented in the middle, but otherwise undamaged. The center was emblazoned with a single winged hawk, the symbol of Korvosa's military. The edge of the shield looked like serrated saw blades, angled upwards and away from the arm that would hold it. He slipped the shield onto my left arm and it clicked into place, the insets humming and then whirring loudly as they screwed it into pre-mounted sockets, though I noticed the connection felt…not insecure. No, it felt as secure as the rest of my armor. But while the armor felt like it would take work for *me* to remove, the shield felt as if it was a mere moment from flying away if I willed it. I tilted my arm to the side and noticed that the underside of the shield was made up of an intricate and complex set of gears and mana crystals, which glowed faintly.

"You can't give her that!" Kessa blurted out.

"Like the Sunder I can't," the armorer frowned. "It has

been a century since Thousand Cutting Calculations died. I can give his saw shield to someone, and this one...I have a *good* feeling about her." He grinned.

He must not have been briefed on my *condition*.

Kessa frowned, but didn't object, as the master armorer started to explain.

"That saw shield has two functions. Three, actually. Firstly, it works as a shield. It's nigh unbreakable...that dent came from the penultimate blow of a power-hammer swung by an enemy champion, a nasty brute from Iana. Bashed the shield aside, then he smashed Calc's defenseless core. You won't have that problem." His gnarled knuckles rapped my breastplate. "Secondly, it's designed to work with your mana cannon. Try powering her up."

I frowned, holding up my left arm. I focused and my hand slipped into my wrist, the shield opened to either side and then folded down. It formed into a boxy shape, mana crystals sticking out of the side and glowing brightly, vents readied to release any built up power and steam safely. There was even an aiming reticule. I focused harder and the mana crystals hummed and shimmered. Energy collected at the barrel that stuck out where my hand had been moments before. Blue-white light started to glow at the tip of the barrel, shimmering and making a loud whirring, winding noise. I grinned.

It took a careful yank *back* to release the mana back into the crystals, which shivered and hissed, steam that smelled strongly of ozone bursting from the vents. The shield clicked back into place and my hand came out. I made a show of looking at my fingernails, saying, "It's all right."

The master armorer snorted. "And finally, you can chuck it."

He gestured, his fingers forming a pattern in the air. A simple spirit had been trained to listen and watch for that, and it caused the left side of the room to open up, revealing three hanging mana-quins, each one shimmering with the marks of being a Suryan soldier. My eyes widened and the master armorer gestured, as if saying: Go nuts.

I wanted to brain him with the shield. I restrained myself, reminding myself: The contract. Just smile, nod, and disembowel your countrymen and you'll get out of this. It helped they were, at the end of the day, just mana-quins.

I bit my lip, then spun on the place, as if I were throwing a discus – a memory guided me, a fuzzy one, barely there, of throwing a disk-grenade while in a trench. The shield launched off my arm, the insets snapping free…but the connection remained, a shimmering thread that I could only see with my Thaumographic vision. The shield roared as it flew through the air, the edge blurring to deadly life as it sheered through three of the targets with a spray of splinters. It roared back, sparking off the wall of the targeting range. My arm lifted of its own accord and the shield snapped back into position, causing me to rock backwards.

"I LIKE IT!"

"It does suit her. Oh! We can add this into the story. She can wrest it from the Sunder, where it's floated for a whole century, waiting for an honored daughter of Korvosa to recover it…" Kessa rubbed her chin. The master armorer picked up one of the beam swords from the pile. He looked it over and I did as well, from a distance. It was a strange feeling. I had never *seen* a beam sword before…and yet, I knew immediately that the hilt design was that of a cutting sword: Tilted at the base, for the ease of handling on spectral horse or auto-cycle, made to help with long slashes rather than thrusts. Of course, my only memory of a swordsman – a regulator from one of the outer islands in Korvosa – hadn't used a cutting sword, he had used a straight sword.

Still, I took the hilt when it was offered, unsure of what it would feel like. None of my past lives had ever wielded a beam sword, but they had all heard of them: Gossamer strands, plucked from the corpses of fairies slain in battle. They were strung into the likeness of a sword and forged in the fires of pure hate. It took a single, dedicated man or woman to forge a beam sword. Someone who could go into the deep Sunder, with nothing but the gossamer strand and still survive. Someone who could focus their rage and hate into a crystalline hilt, carved to suit the hand of a Champion and obey their will.

The gossamer would then transmute into solid light, which poured itself into the hilt...and waited to emerge. Beam swords didn't just cut: They *burned.* They were *eager* to fight, to spill blood: Dreamlike fairie blood, the ichor of the Nameless, red human blood or the glowing mana blood of a Champion, it didn't matter.

My hand closed around the hilt offered by the master armorer. I shivered – my hand buzzed – and I could hear the distant, thumping noises, the sound of drums. War drums.

I tapped the blade on.

There was a sound of the air itself cleaving as the blade sprang free: A bright, blood red. The ruby light shimmered and I saw the clear shape of the cutting sword – the name that came to mind was the gladius, but I knew that was at least a hundred years out of date, maybe more. But it fit: A brutal, fierce name. A name of hacked off limbs.

I tapped the blade off and it quieted.

"I think she's ready." The master armorer murmured.

"She's not even close to ready," Kessa said.

"She is also still present," I said. "And self-aware, even. I might, and this is just me going out on a limb here, have a heroic soul which has reincarnated many times in service of S...the nation." I looked at the two of them. Kessa and the master armorer looked abashed.

"Of course, Champion." Kessa curtsied. "Now, I was in discussion with the weavers about your costumes, and we've narrowed the options down to two, but I know you're going to take option one."

"Oh?" I cocked an eyebrow. "And what if I demanded option two, just to be contrarian?"

"Then you'll be stuck with this." She held up a scroll she had been hiding behind her back. It unfurled to show me – well, me if I had huge boobs and was dressed up in the most insanely sexified uniform I could imagine. It looked like the standard gray-green and black cut of a Korvosan naval officer's outfit, but with a Champion's logo on the shoulder and...well, the midriff was exposed and the bust was emphasized with the cut.

I blinked.

"Option one, and the one I'm pushing for, well, you'll be spending most of your time either in this," She gestured to the armor. "Or in the simple stuff you were wearing earlier. Nothing too revealing or exotic."

I blinked. "So...people will actually think of me as a warrior instead of a sex object?" I was honestly shocked.

"That and when we bring out the pinups, they'll be even MORE impressive: 45C, under the hood!" She held out her hands, as if pressing a saucy pin-up poster to the wall. "That'll really catch their attention."

I closed my eyes, rubbing my temple with a gauntleted finger.

Kessa patted my shoulder, comfortingly. "Oh, come on. Everything else about you is artifice. The whole world is artifice. If you want reality..." She trailed off. I knew she had been about to say: Go to the Sunder, but she didn't need to. The master armorer was there, studiously working on a piece of equipment for some other Champion, ignoring me completely now that he had armored me up.

I sighed. "I know..." I said. "It's just...I just want to help people, okay? I just want to fight bad guys and make life safer for everyone."

Well, for Suryans. But, well, who was really the bad

guy in this situation? Was it the every-day Korvosan Populat worker in the factory, the man or woman who lived for the daily tapestry opera, just to take their mind off the eternal work shifts that it took to keep a nation from collapsing into the Sunder? Those people had to have the Champions. As axiomatic symbols of the State, Champions could become the focal point for imagination and creativity. The people *needed* us to keep everything from falling apart. Were they so evil to want us to be, at the very least, interesting?

No.

They deserved protection too.

I sighed, softly. My eyes closed. When they opened, I looked at Kessa.

"So, uh…maybe the love triangle can be…between a girl and a boy? To have wider…appeal?"

Kessa smiled an actual smile, one that wasn't born of glee in some new merchandising kick. She patted my shoulder. "I'll take it under advisement."

Chapter 3: Meet the Champions

"And this is the dormitory!"

Kessa gestured with a single hand, encompassing what looked like a great many rooms that I had both seen and not seen before – and some that I had heard of and not heard of as well. It was weird, the sense of removal from my own knowledge. The curved loft along the top of the room looked like it was straight out of a Ularian collegisia, while the refractory that was settled in the left hand corner, between the stairwells that led up to the loft itself, looked as if it had been plucked out of the hundreds of militat camps that my past lives had eaten in. But the decorations? Those were straight from a memory of a memory: Past lives dreams of opulent mansions, given gaudy reality that…that…just felt *wrong*.

I didn't deserve to have rooms with jade walls and filigree and murals and living tapestries. I looked at Kessa, about to object, when I met the first fellow member of my Cogwheel. He walked out of one of the doors on the loft, down the stairs and into the refractory. Once there, he yanked the quintessence-receptacle open and rummaged around, bent over with his back facing us, and fished out a jug of glowing mana-infused sky goat milk. He started to drink straight from the carton, scratching his butt.

And he was completely naked.

"Home of the brave, deadly, incredibly well trained and disciplined Korvosan Champions, right?" I asked, glancing at Kessa, who had just slapped her palm over her face.

The Champion had a different cast to his skin next to Stern and me; rather than blue or gray-green, his skin was a bright, shimmering gold, the golden of orichalicum or imagined sunlight. His implants only showed in the tiny blue gemstones set in his temples, a few circuits and wires connecting them to the back of his head – making him look like he had a two pairs of dreadlocks – the wires and the obsidian crystal hanging from his head. And, most glaringly, his left hand, which was almost twice as big as his right hand and rather than being made out of clay, it was articulated steel and hissing brass pistons and gimbals and rubberized tubes.

He turned, glowing milk dripping from his chin as he gaped at me and Kessa, and froze. His eyes went wide.

Silence, save for the drip drip drip of the milk and the faint *whirr* of his eyes focusing on us.

"*Well-Lubricated Cognitive Engine*…put on some godsdamn pants." Kessa's voice sounded muffled from behind her palm.

"Right." He started to shuffle away from the stasis-box, covering himself with his large hand. He put the empty carton down on the shelf that ringed the kitchen, paused, and then turned and ran so fast that I almost didn't see him get to the door and vanish inside.

"Good name. Accurate," I said, nodding slightly.

"Engi is usually a bit scattered, but he's also the smartest member of the team," Kessa said. "Honest."

"Oh, no, I totally believe you," I said. "Smart people regularly forget their pants."

Kessa glared at me. A few seconds later, Engi came out of the door. He was wearing pants now – simple, homespun black leather pants – and he skipped down the stairs, his over-large hand scraping on the banister. He walked over, offering his right hand to me with a shy grin.

"Sorry about that! Uh, I'm-"

"*Well-Lubricated Cognitive Engine*, I got it the first time," I smiled, slightly, taking his hand and shaking it carefully. "I'm Cee."

"Cee?"

"Cee." I said. "Or, did you want my full designation?"

"It's *Vengeful Crystalline Hawk 45C*," Kessa interjected. "She'll be your Cogwheel's muscle and aerial support. Sorry about her not being here for your group orientation, but her construction took a few days longer than expected."

The lie that we had agreed on. Each Champion took a different amount of time to build and quicken, so a Cogwheel was usually kept apart, until they could all be brought together as one. It wasn't *exactly* a perfect reason for why I had spent the days normally spent meeting the rest of the Cogwheel in a prison cell. But it would just have to do for now.

"Oh fantastic!" Engi bought it. Clearly, intelligent people were also really dumb sometimes. "Doc will be happy that we'll have someone who can handle Sunder threats without having to use a war kite or a sky ship or something. Oh, Doc is our leader."

"I'd have thought he was some kind of doctor." I said, frowning.

"It's short for *Doctrine Proves Itself.*" Kessa interjected.

"Of course it is." I shook my head.

"So, are you just about melee combat?" Engi asked, gesturing me over to the kitchen. "Oh, have you eaten anything? Do you need to top off your mana batteries?"

"I've only used a bit of mana, so, I think I'm okay."

"All right." He grinned, sitting down at a stool, his

large hand tapping on the countertop. "Oh! So, do you want to meet the rest of the team? Oh, and, um, when you do, can you refrain from mentioning my lack of pants?"

"You weren't wearing PANTS!?" A squeaky, child-like voice chirruped from the countertop. I glanced and saw a huge, ugly, horrifying looking red and black spider. I screamed and slammed my hand down on it, crushing it with a loud CLANG! Gears and sparks flew in every direction from under my hand. I jerked my hand back, looking at the twitching, smoking ruin of the spider. A yelp came from one of the other rooms.

"Ooooh boy." Engi sighed.

The door opened…and a wave of spiders skittered out. It was the single most horrifying thing I had ever seen, a chittering, clicking hoard of steel and brass, moving with unnatural speed and clicking precision. The spiders swarmed over the wall, the ground, then started to climb on top of one another, legs interlocking, bodies merging together. They created a horrifying approximation of a humanoid form, then secreted a silvery mithril coating, which firmed then sculpted itself into a slender, knife thin girl with long, silver hair and dark black eyes. She was slightly hunched and hid her face behind her curtain of silvery hair, so that only one of her eyes was visible.

"Please don't do that." Her voice was very soft as she

picked up the smooshed spider.

"S-Sorry," I stammered.

She dissolved into spiders and then the swarm flowed back into the room.

I shuddered and gagged.

"And that's *Spy-Dar 4331*." Engi said. "You get used to her."

"*Spy-Dar 4331*?" I asked. "And, wait, I thought Champions have to be made out of clay. She…where's the clay on her?"

"She's a prototype. We all are, in some way. My prototype part is this-" He hefted his hand. "I don't know what yours is, but-"

"My insets." I cut in. "They make the armor lighter, so I can fly while wearing super heavy plate mail."

He nodded. "Well, Spy is the first Champion whose soul is imbued into something with a minimum of clay. Doc is the first Champion…well…maybe you should meet him first." He stroked his chin. "But he's sleeping."

"We need sleep? I thought Champions don't sleep," I asked.

"Everyone thinks that," Engi said. "I thought that too. It's part of the media, the legend, you know? But no, Champions need sleep for the same reasons humans need sleep. It refreshes our connection to the Eye." He shrugged. "Mortals that go without sleep, well, you know what happens to them."

I nodded, my face grim. It wasn't exactly a pleasant thing to think of. Some nations – the Forsaken Nations – used those kinds of people as living bombs. It wasn't that hard to implant a piece of magitech into a brain to keep someone awake. They'd go to their day job, then head home and rather than sleep, they would think about their true nation and wait for the moment where the Eye finally turned its gaze from them. That moment was when they lost their name.

The Autarch had *dared* to call my past life a terrorist. Anyone who might do that, anyone who might make a Nameless, just to hit back at their enemies, that was a *real* terrorist. Nameless were bad enough in the Sunder, but in a civilized region, they were nightmare incarnate – writhing tentacles, given plentiful reality to devour, and souls to rip apart, to feed themselves and grow even stronger.

"A Champion becoming Nameless is too scary to think of. Ever heard legends of Re'kar?"

"Several of my lives have. The Mother of the Nameless," I said.

"I have a theory that Re'kar is actually a Champion who went Nameless…"

Kessa coughed, loudly. We had both completely forgotten her and she was looking at me with exasperation. "Cee, I'm glad you're hitting it off with your teammates, literally in Spy's case, but we do need you to meet *Doctrine Proves Itself* as soon as possible."

"Fine, fine." I stood up, then smiled at Engi. Despite his initial impression, he…was actually kinda nice. He smiled back at me and I realized that maybe, just maybe, I might do good with this Cogwheel.

Turns out I might be wrong. I hated *Doctrine Proves Itself*. The reason was pretty simple: He was a stuck up, pompous, jackbooted Korvosan ass and seemed to enjoy proving it every single sentence.

"I don't like the idea of incorporating a Suryan terrorist into our unit," he said, stroking his chin.

"I'm under freaking CONTRACT!" I said. "And I wasn't a *terrorist*. I was a *freedom fighter*."

Kessa – who sat between us at the conference table – leaned forward, looking at me, then at Doc. "Doctrine, 45C has been entirely cooperative, if a bit…acerbic."

"Thanks!"

"That's not a compliment." Kessa frowned at me before looking back at Doc. "But she's also an investment that the Korvosan government can't very well throw away or give to another nation. Can you please at least make an *effort?*"

Doc pursed his lips. He was, like Engi, a clay-based Champion, but unlike Engi, his implants gave his voice the timber and resonance that had made Stern sound so very likable and worthy of respect. Doc didn't have the same effortless knack that Stern had, but the foundation was there. He wore a simple but effective uniform of a gold and black cut, complete with a militat leader's epaulets, enhancing the martial bearing of him. The coloration matched his silver hued skin, highlighted with thin lines of gold that surrounded his jawline – pulsating with tiny flickers of mana with every word.

For anyone else, that uniform might have made him seem like a natural leader.

For me, it just harkened back to the same jackbooted thugs who had marched through the home town of my core memory.

"You claim you were not a terrorist, Cee, and yet you listed one of your talents as making IEDs out of improvised magical materials." He frowned. "You claim that you want to work with me, and yet, you admit that you only work because you're under contract. I don't need a mind-bent slave, I need an actual *Champion.*"

I snarled, standing up. "Actual Champion!? You-"

"Cee!" Kessa yelped.

"And you have anger control issues," Doc added.

"No, I just can't stand talking to Korvosan thugs."

He frowned at me. He managed to focus his disapproval almost like a weapon. For a moment, I felt chagrined to *death*, a decidedly unpleasant feeling. Then a sneaking suspicion led me to cut through the disapproval by activating my Thaumographic sight. I saw that he was trickling mana into gemstones mounted on his chakra. The bastard was using an implant to augment his frown! Brainwashing son of a bitch. I glared right back at him, clenching my fingers on the table so hard that it started to deform.

He narrowed his eyes slightly but didn't say anything immediately.

"I also don't need magic to make people agree with me." I growled.

"People agree with you?"

"You'll agree with my fist. In your face."

"That doesn't even make sense."

Kessa closed her eyes and started to rub her temples.

I looked at Kessa, then at Doctrine. I could practically see my own junking and recycling on his expression. With his charisma and his implants, I was fairly sure that he could talk circles around anyone who might object to his request that I get moved off the Cogwheel. That meant no more Cee, no more hope of getting to Surya, no nothing.

I breathed in. This was going to be hard. This was going to be hard and painful. But this was going to be necessary, if I wanted to live to see the end of the contract. I gritted my teeth and forced the words out with the breath I had taken. "*Doctrine Proves Itself*, I am sorry for my outburst. I will work with you. I want to get back to Surya...but I also want to help people. Korvosan citizens don't have a choice that they were born here. That doesn't mean that I can leave them in the lurch and not protect them from Nameless or Fairies."

Doc tapped a single finger on the table for a few moments. Kessa looked at me in something approximating absolute shock followed by actual hope.

Doc nodded. "Very well. But if you endanger this team with your Suryan loyalty, then I will have *Dedicated Panoply 998-Alpha* restrain you and I will personally see you court-martialed."

"I assume she's the fifth member of the team. And that she is badass enough to...restrain me without help."

"...badass is not *quite* the right word for it," he said, smirking slightly. "But still, I believe that we might be able to work you into the group after all. Somewhere in there..."

"I'm so very glad." I managed to speak without grinding my teeth into pieces.

"Let us begin, then."

Doctrine stood and walked towards the door. It hissed open and I saw Kessa look like she was about to melt into a puddle of relief. I walked past her, my wings folded tight behind my back.

"Try to win Doctrine over, please," she whispered.

I looked at her as if she had gone insane. Sighing, Kessa expanded.

"Even if you're under contract, and even if you promise to work with him, that doesn't follow then that he won't not like you. I mean, it isn't like you're actually *working* at being likable-"

"I am trying!" I said, wounded.

"Try harder." She frowned at me. "If Doctrine doesn't *use* you in a fight properly, because he doesn't feel like he can rely on your combat skills because you two don't get along JUST because you're a Suryan terrorist, then people will die. Get along with him, or I will write the worst backstory for you." Her finger prodded my chest, alarmingly. "The. Worst."

I looked at her finger, then at her. She was...right. Doctrine was the team leader, and while I didn't know his full load out, he surely had some kind of tactical implants that would help him lead us in a battle, if nowhere else. I looked from her to the door, where Doc stood, tapping his foot impatiently.

I looked back at Kessa.

"I'll try," I said, my voice soft. She narrowed her eyes, then nodded slowly, seeming to take my word for it. With that, she slapped my shoulder, pushing me (well, trying to push me) towards the door. I relented, hurrying out with Doctrine.

As he led me along, Doctrine filled the corridor with his voice – which, at the very least, was not boring to listen to. He also had a habit of gesturing, and the gemstones implanted into his fingertips would flicker to life, projecting moving images, usually ones related to whatever he was talking about: In this case, *Dedicated Panoply 998-Alpha*.

She looked like a normal Champion's body augmented and extended out into something almost three times larger than normal. Her legs had been opened up and had bracers and extenders placed in, with a secondary pair of legs that thrust out behind her, giving her a square gait. Her torso had a framework of cold iron and steel, and a protective carapace that looked almost bug-like with five arms. Two of them were heavy mounts and were both on the right side of the body with a smaller third arm stuck between them. The other two were more normal sized and mounted on the front to the left and right – leaving her rather lopsided looking. The 'forward' arms were mounted on a set of gimbals which themselves were mounted on a rotating circlet, allowing them to rotate a full 360 degrees, giving her some chance to manipulate normal objects.

"Pan is our long-ranged support and emergency transport fallback." Doc pointed to the legs. "In a pinch, those can be modified by Engi to produce gravitic lift and carry us all out of trouble."

I nodded.

"Her full loadout is going to be a super-sized vortex bow, fifty vortex arrows, and two-man portable mana cannons slung off the front."

I whistled. Memories of what a normal sized vortex bow could do were burned into all my soldier memories: Screaming people, sucked into miniature Eyes, their bodies ripped apart and their souls chucked back into the reincarnation cycle without so much as a by your leave. It was a bit more merciful than a soulcidian blade – which would drink a soul into its obsidian surface and keep it there forever – but souls so ripped apart tended to enter their next lives with Pre-Incarnation Stress Disorder.

We came to a doorway, which hissed open and

revealed a huge, cavernous room with a padded floor and…Panoply. She had been scary big in a living image. In person, even from about twenty feet away, she was *terrifyingly* gargantuan. Her legs thumped and whirred as she stepped backwards, her torso hissing and clicking as it turned around to track a flying target, her vortex bow strung and cocked with her two huge arms. The arm holding the string released and the mock arrow pinned the target to the wall with a CRUNCH. That arm cocked the string back and the smaller third arm snapped an arrow into position.

Three targets flew out.

CRUNCH! CRUNCH! CRUNCH!

"Her rate of fire is pretty good, huh?" Doc murmured, his shoulders straightening and drawing up – patriotism writ large across his face. "That's a fine example of Korvosan engineering…a true Champion."

"Eh, she's pretty good." I said, trying to not sound impressed.

"Yes, yes, she really is…" Doctrine's voice had a faintly far away air to it. I looked at him – at his face – and then at Pan, then at him. I grinned, feeding a bit of mana into my Thaumographic Spirit Sight Eyes.

"Someone has a cruuuuuush!" I said, in a sing-song voice.

"What!?" Doctrine's high pitched squeak sounded even funnier due to the complete lack of magitechnologically imprinted supernatural charisma. "I...I do not!"

Noticing us, Pan waved with her manipulator arms, thumping over, holstering her bow into a slot mounted on her back. "Hi snoogums! I mean, uh-"

Doc scowled at Pan, his arms crossed over his chest. She didn't seem very remorseful – though, that was hard to tell as her body had no real head. A circular port opened at the bottom of her torso. What looked like a humanoid figure dropped down out of her main combat chassis: Pan's humanoid form was decidedly under developed compared to most Champions. Her only implants were the mountings on her shoulders. Oh, and her body ended at her hips. Rather than legs, she had a single large Glorious Soaring Conduction Array Gemstone Platform which kept her floating about two feet off the ground with an eerie humming noise. She wore a vest that seemed to be made entirely out of blue tubes and metal blocks hooked together in a wild, chaotic pattern. Heating vanes opened on her back, glowing a bright red and releasing a spray of superheated steam.

"Sorry, sorry," she said. "What's up, Doctrine?"

"This is *Vengeful Crystalline Hawk 45C*, our melee

combatant and flying specialist." Doc gestured to me. I shook Pan's hand. She felt *incredibly* hot.

"That rig has to be really energy intensive…"

"Yeah, a bit." She shrugged. "It has inbuilt mana generators, but the excess heat has to be filtered through me, hence my cool-down vest and heater vanes. Neat, huh?" She gestured to her vest, and I saw the tubes weren't blue; they were *filled* with blue fluid, which rushed through and around her body. She clapped her hands, drawing my attention back to her. "Oh! I should show you the Endbomb!"

"The Endbomb?"

She floated over to me, bumping her hip against mine as she gestured her arms out wide, speaking excitedly. "Imagine a bomb to end all bombs…"

Doc coughed. "Pan."

"A bomb that can only be launched from a specially designed cannon!"

"Pan."

"A bomb that doesn't just explode and doesn't just implode, but does *both*. At the same *time*."

"Pan."

"Yes, snoog…Doctrine?" She asked, before whispering to me. "Oh, also, it can be set to stun."

I nodded. Double take. "Wait, what?"

Doc frowned but chose to ignore Pan's near slipup. "Cee will be doing the up close and personal damage while you will be bringing down the thunder at range. Do you two want to arrange some extra training time together?"

I looked at Pan, then nodded. She gave me two thumbs up, though her cheeks were still darkened in a blush.

"Very good. I will be back in fifteen minutes. Have a schedule ready and congruent with the schedule you already have, Cee," he said, freighting his words with enough magical energy to practically sear them into my brain. I could feel my thought spiders scrambling to back them up. I scowled, knowing that I would be remembering them in the shower for the rest of the week.

This was a weird thought, since the thought of me, in the shower, thinking of Doc's orders for the rest of the week...that didn't come from experience, not my experience. I mean, I hadn't even *had* a shower. In my whole life. But I knew the feel of water sliding along my back, and the aggravating mortification of bursting into the same irritating pop-song that I had been humming all week while I was...

I shook my head, the haze of memories darting away, leaving Pan looking at me, concern.

"Sorry," I said. "Just trying to get used to being Cee. I

mean, do you get that feeling? Like-"

"Like you're young and old, and know everything and nothing. Like, you should still be sitting around picking your nose and being burped and fed on milk, but you can list off the names and dates of the entire history of the Sunder, from the Endwar to the Champion Era?" She asked, floating backwards as she did so, holding her hands out wide. "Yeah. Yeah, we kind of all feel that…" She smiled. "At least you don't have any weird emotional things going on to screw with *your* training."

I wanted to reply. But I didn't – I wasn't sure if the contract would twig at that, but I didn't want to risk it.

"When I woke up, the first person I met was my social engineer, and she introduced me to my Warform," Pan said, patting the leg of her larger body. "But then, part way through, Doctrine walks in…" She blushed. "A-and…and I feel something, right here." She patted her chest, where he heart would have been, if she had been a mortal. "I feel like something started and stopped at the same time."

I blinked, then used my Thaumographic eye to see that her aura was, if anything, even more tinged with the flickering reds and blues of love, the tendrils working deeper and further into her than they had for Doc.

"Two lifetimes ago, I was a man and he was a woman,

and we loved each other very much. He...she died leading a charge through open Sunder into Ianer trenches. Then, I, that is, my incarnation, met him, that is, her again, but that time, she was a he, and..." She shook her head, flushing. "My incarnation fell in love again! And, do you know what the engineers said when they noted that connection while they were building us?"

I stepped over, putting my hand on her shoulder. I had to blink rapidly to prevent my eyes from going completely out of alignment for some stupid reason which I completely didn't understand. I wiped at my cheek, and it was wet. My eyes were malfunctioning. Without a doubt.

"They said it was irrelevant. They said that they only cared about my incarnation's artillery skills and his incarnation's tactical acumen." Pan made a face. "Oh, by the Dead Gods, we've just met and already I'm spilling my multi-generational sob story to you, I am so sorry. This is *completely* unprofessional."

"No, it's okay," I said. "I mean, it's not like you've gotten a chance to learn to filter."

Pan put her hands over her mouth, trying to prevent a giggle from escaping. She slid her fingers away from her lips, and said: "It's okay, though. I mean, we're Champions, we're working together! We should be friends."

Kessa was *totally* going to say 'I told you so.'

"Awesome. You seem cool! We should work out a good practice schedule, so I can shoot the bad guys without also killing you," Pan said, floating with me over towards a table set near the wall. There, we got to work. The schedule that we both had been given for our shared training was pretty brutal –beam sword usage, thaumaturgic theory, proper tactics and strategy, public relations, speech giving, and other things, all of them stacked together with our superhuman constitutions considered, meaning the actual free time to slot additional training was fairly rare, at least until the crunch of early training was over.

"So, uh, why snoogums?" I asked as we found another hour-long break in the schedule to fit some training time together.

"What? Oh!" Pan blushed, her greenish skin darkening further. "It just pops out."

I nodded, and we went back to work.

Once we finished, Doc returned, and I took my fourth…no, fifth look at him. A lot of reevaluations were going on today – all really fast. I wondered if that had anything to do with being a few days old.

On this fifth look, I saw just how hard Doctrine was

working to *look* in charge. And when I used my Thaumographic sight, I saw that his aura had dampened down and been concealed by some kind of shrouding implant. Was he just hiding his feelings for Pan? Or fear at not being good enough to lead?

"This looks quite good!" He said. I frowned at the note of surprise in his voice.

"Awesome," Pan said. "Now, I should get back to my own training, right?"

Doctrine nodded but didn't make eye contact with her.

"Yes, Sir!" Pan floated backwards, getting underneath her rig. She shot straight up, the rig closing around her.

Doc faced me. "Do you want to see your quarters, Cee?"

I nodded. Some sleeping would help me settle.

"All right!" Pan floated backwards, getting underneath her rig, waving as she did so. She shot straight up, the rig closing around her. Pan's Warform rumbled to life and she stretched. "Oh, so you know, the rooms are pretty nice, Cee."

She turned, sliding her bow out of her slot. I turned to go, walking with Doc, my face pensive.

"I have a question!" Pan said. We both turned toward her. "Do you sleep on your belly or your side?"

"I've only been activated for a few days," I said,

smiling a bit. "And I slept in the lotus position because my cell didn't have a bed."

"Cell?"

"Come on, Cee." Doc said, hurriedly. He added a bit of a crack to his words, mana trickling along his vocal cords to make his words nearly irresistible. He led me back to the main room, then took me to a door built into the side of the loft – it was next to Spy's room and across from Engi's. He opened it and gestured me into the room.

"This is where you'll be sleeping, resting, relaxing, reading." He said. "If you have any questions, I am sure that your social engineers can answer them for you." He frowned. "However, they will be unavailable for the next few hours."

"Why?"

"Because I need to speak with them to design a stratagem for including you into the team's promotional material." Doc sighed and for a moment, I actually felt sorry and grateful for him. He nodded to me, turned, and left the room. Once the door closed, I noticed an armor rack that sat empty in the corner of the room. I stepped over to that, standing in the position indicated by the glyph, and automatic-arms whirred out to grab onto my armor. Then, it was just a matter of withdrawing mana from my insets. The armor became heavy, then was slipped off me by the arms. I stepped forward, stretching out my wings and arms, sighing.

My uniform waited for me on the bed. I slipped it on, adjusting it for a moment, and then started to really poke around the place. There was a small planter in the corner of the room and a window that looked out over the capitol of Korvosa and the Sunder beyond. And, last but far from least, there was a living tapestry. I tapped it on and the tapestry stitched itself into a holding pattern. I tapped my chin, unsure of what to do next. I noticed two toggles with a series of glyphs: ADULT, ROMANCE, COMEDY, ACTION, HORROR. The other had only two options: CHAMPION and HUMAN.

I toggled through them. Human Action was propaganda: Heroic Korvosans battling lying Lycanshian's, manipulative Suryans, intellectual but ineffectual Uylarians and so on. Champion Action was currently showing *Stern Hand of Industry* battling Nameless, his mighty hands closing around the wriggling, almost formless bodies and squeezing the un-life out of them. The glyphs claimed this was reenactments of a historic battle. I spent a few moments marveling at the fidelity and grace of the stich work and the movement of the fake Nameless. My core memories remembered seeing moving tapestries, where monsters that were not actually there had no depth or foreshadowing, standing out starkly against the more realistic human and Champion actors.

Of course, tapestries in my day had had no color.

I shook my head, turning the tapestry off.

"What a brave new world." I muttered to myself.

Then, remembering Pan's question, I sat down on the bed and tried laying on my back.

It wasn't comfortable.

I tried laying on my side.

It wasn't comfortable.

I tried laying on my belly.

That wasn't comfortable either. Then, I placed a pillow under my breasts in just the right place, then another pillow where my head could rest on it…that worked. I closed my eyes, and slowly reviewed in my mind everything that had happened today. Everything that had happened in my life.

It was a depressingly short amount of time, considering I could – if I focused – remember snippets from the trenches a thousand years before: Standing atop the parapet, sword raised, an army at my back, howling my name. But I couldn't *remember* the name. I couldn't even remember the colors of the army. Was it Korvosan? Or was it some other nation, from the dim times between the Endwar and the founding of the Nations? All that I remembered was the *feeling* of the speech, spilling from my mouth, the feeling of the grand gestures, the knowledge that I would have a thousand men dying for me, for my cause.

I could remember crawling through the rubble of Surya, the dream fragments of blasted homes, the whispering Sunder-fog that crept in when reality fields were cracked by vortex bombardment and by mana-cascades. I could remember this and the arguments with legates in a Hall of Justice – the arguments it took to wring some actual justice out of the Korvosan justice system. I frowned, my eyes opening as I rubbed my temple with one of my fingers. That...

I had *won* cases. I had gotten innocent people off of crimes they had not committed.

There had been justice there. But not in the rubble of my hometown.

I scowled at the wall. Pan struggled with unrequited, unwanted love, picked up because her soul had the memories of an artillerist. I struggled with loyalty, because they had needed a soul with the skills of sword and speech and archery and all the bits of knowledge that *they* had needed. Korvosa.

"Just like a Korvosan, isn't it?" I asked the wall.

Isn't it?

Justice in the courts, won through words – public speaking. Bodies, strung up at gallows, with signs nailed to their chests in simplified glyphics: *Partisan.*

I was a partisan.

I was a Korvosan, Suryan, legate, partisan, swordswoman, archer, martial artist.

I was a Champion.

The thought made me relax, ever so slightly, my head resting forward against the bed. I closed my eyes and listened, for the moment to my thought spiders crawling about inside of my head. If I was a Champion first, then…what was I second? Was I anything second? Was I just a collection of memories and thoughts, walking around in a weapon of magical mass destruction.

No. That was just the fear talking. The fear that I was wrong, that my memories were wrong, that my whole life – my life crawling through the dream rubble, my life spent lining up a crossbow sights on a Korvosan soldier as he picked his way past what had been my hometown – had been spent for nothing. That fear was wrong. Surya meant more than just…anger. It meant more than just hating Korvosans because they were from Korvosa. It meant respect for liberty, for freedom of expression, for the democratic rule of law.

I closed my wings on my back, and made my decision.

I was a Champion of Surya, not Korvosa. But that meant that Korvosa was just going to get my own special brand of help, and it was going to appreciate it.

Even if it didn't know it yet.

I smiled, and felt all of my memories – the memories of flashing blades and flying kicks, of hissing arrows and the grumbling roar of mana cannon artillery, of the shouted words of kings and priests, gods and men – settle and click firmly into place.

I was *Vengeful Crystalline Hawk 45C.*

And I was going to kick ass.

I curled up around my pillow, closed my eyes tightly, and then sent the word to my thought spiders. They flicked a switch.

I fell asleep.

About the Author:

David Colby – bereft of anything actually interesting in his life – has dedicated his life to writing exciting stories set in fantastical locations. There are often lasers – such as in his one published novel, Debris Dreams!

Find out more about this artist:

http://quantumspinplates.blogspot.com/

Dust

by Danielle DeVor

The sticky-tape was coming up off the floor again. She would need to fix it tomorrow when it was safe to go into town. Nothing walked around in the daylight anymore. Well, nothing except for her that is.

The sticky-tape was loud when you walked across it. Loud was important. So few things made noise that didn't have to be powered by electricity. But, remembering helped nothing. She needed to concentrate on now—not before.

Sticky-tape, batteries, food. So far, that was all that was on tomorrow's list. It helped her block out the thumps on the house from outside.

"Manda!"

She threw her hands up over her ears to block out the sound. She didn't need to remember him. Not now.

She got up from her chair and poked at the fire in the fireplace. She was always cold, so it was best not to let it go out completely. Otherwise, she'd have to freeze until morning. Going out with THEM around was suicide.

"Manda!"

There was a louder thud against the front door. The

mirror must have broken again. Something else to add to the list. Mirror, sticky-tape, batteries, food. The list was growing.

She sat back down in the chair and kept her hands in her lap.

She glanced at the clock. Only five more hours to go until light. She could do it.

Suddenly, she jerked awake. The fire was barely embers.

"Shit! Shit! Shit!"

She jumped up from the chair and stabbed at the fire with the poker. She added the last log to what was left. After a moment, it caught. She took a deep breath and let the poker fall to the floor. It had been close. Another addition to the list. Wood, mirror, sticky-tape, batteries, food.

"Manda!"

The thud cracked the doorjamb this time. She'd known he'd eventually find her. She'd just hoped there would have been more time than this. She hopped up from the chair and grabbed the loose cabinet door she'd removed from the kitchen earlier that day. Then, she grabbed the three nails she had left on the stand and a hammer.

"Manda!"

She crept over to the front door. Her hands were

shaking so hard she feared she would drop the cabinet door. She forced herself to still and hammered it into place over the front door jamb right above the lock. That way, it would have more support. As soon as she was finished, she looked up at the clock. Four-thirty. It was almost over.

"Manda!"

And, another thud, but the door held fast. She went back over toward the fire, picked up the poker, and stoked the fire for a minute. Then, she leaned the poker up against the fireplace and went back over to her chair and sat down.

Before, everything had been so perfect. She'd met Jason at a carnival months ago. His brown hair and green eyes seemed magical in the sunlight. But, this was long before THEY came. Monsters were the creatures in movies back then, not roaming around on the streets.

Too bad Jason hadn't listened. She thought he would have understood, but she'd been wrong. The rules always kept you safe. She should know, but she'd made the mistake of breaking one.

The log popped on the fire. She jumped.

"Manda!"

Another thud against the door. There was a new cracking sound. Her heart hammered in her chest. She had nothing else to secure the door with. The clock now read four-forty-five. If the door would just hold for a little longer.

Nails, wood, mirror, sticky-tape, batteries, food.

Soon, the thudding stopped. Light began to creep below the curtains and around the slats she'd nailed up over the windows.

Since she'd already slept, she put on her shoes and prepared to go out.

When the light was fully up in the sky, she crept through the garage and stepped out the side door. The mirror was still intact over there.

She hopped onto her bicycle and headed to town. It didn't take long to collect most of the things she needed. Food was always the hardest to find, but once found, she went ahead and filled her stomach before heading back home.

Once there, she set about securing the house again. She even hammered new nails into the front door to secure it better. She knew she needed a new one, but a door would be too hard to carry by herself. So, she'd just have to make do.

So far, the only thing on tomorrow's list was food, but the day was early.

#

"Manda!"

"Dammit, boy. That didn't work yesterday and it sure as hell ain't gonna work now. Just get out of the way."

Jason watched as his dad put the make-shift battering ram into position in front of the door.

"I don't want to do this," Jason said.

His dad stared at him. "That's just fine. You want to explain to Carl why his daughter's death ain't gonna be avenged?"

Jason looked down at the ground. "No, sir."

His dad grunted. "That's what I thought."

Jason raised his head and watched his father turn toward the others in their posse. "Remember, these things are blind in the sunlight, boys. We get that door open and that thing is ours!"

"Dad?"

His father groaned. "What?"

"How do you know she's blind?"

The man put his hand on Jason's shoulder. "All nightwalkers are blind in the sunlight. Looks black to them so I've heard. Day to us looks like night to them and vice versa."

"That's so weird."

The man nodded. "It was sheer dumb luck she confided in you, boy."

"I really liked her."

"That's the power of the beast, boy. They make you want'em. Remember this day as a warning. No more lollygagging after dark."

"Yes, sir."

"Good boy." He stared at the motor on the machine. "Ready?"

He didn't wait for an answer and propelled the machine forward. The ram broke through the door, sending splinters in all directions. There was a scream within the house that sounded like a demonic bird of prey.

"Go get'em, tiger," Jason's dad said.

Jason saluted his father. "Yes, sir."

Then, he stormed inside. He found her in the chair by the door, arms shielding herself from the impending attack. Her blond hair was stringy and dirty in the sunlight. When he'd seen her months ago at night, she'd seemed beautiful. Now, she was something foul. "Manda?"

She came up out of that chair with a snarl. Her pointed teeth dripping with saliva.

Jason pulled his pistol from his holster and shot her once in the middle of the forehead. Before she could recover from what should be a mortal wound, he dragged her out into the yard.

"Good boy," his father said.

"Still can't believe she was one of them."

His dad sauntered over and severed her head from her body with an axe. "Look at it this way, boy. Another one bites the dust."

"Amen."

About the Author:

Named one of the Examiner's 2014 Women in Horror: 93 Horror Authors you Need to Read Right Now, Danielle DeVor has been spinning the spider webs, or rather, the keyboard for more frights and oddities. She spent her early years fantasizing about vampires and watching "Salem's Lot" way too many times. When not writing and reading about weird things, you will find her hanging out at the nearest coffee shop, enjoying a mocha Frappuccino.

Find out more about this artist:
https://danielledevor.wordpress.com/

Dallying with Dodecapus
by Lita Kurth

The café was about to close.

"I'll bet you the cost of my lunch you can't," he said, not even looking at her. "You're on."

He wore a hateful gray suit as if he didn't know what gray meant around here and glanced out the glass doors. "Really?" His voice, too, was gray. Why had she even fed him?

"Watch." She folded and unfolded ten of her arms, demonstrating that she could indeed pick up twenty-five bowls using the suction cups on the inside of her elbows.

He frowned.

"What's the matter?" All four of her eyebrows furled in a menacing way.

He flicked a crumb from his sleeve. "Using suction cups is cheating."

"So I cheat." She reached over and suctioned his eyeballs out of his head.

About the Author:

Lita Kurth (MFA Pacific Lutheran University) has had work published in Fjords Review, Brain, Child, Main Street Rag, Tikkun, NewVerseNews, Blast Furnace, Raven Chronicles, ellipsis…literature and art, Compose, Redux, Chicago Literati, Composite Arts, Verbatim Poetry, the Santa Clara Review, Gyroscope Review, Vermont Literary Review, DNA-Dragonfly Press, Defenestration, Draft: a Journal of Process, Trash Fiction, Tattoo Highway, and others.

Her CNF, "Pivot," was nominated for a Pushcart Prize. Her CNF "This is the Way We Wash the Clothes," presented at the Working Class Studies conference, 2012, won the 2014 Diana Woods Memorial Award (summer-fall 2014) and appeared in Lunchticket 2014.

She contributes to Tikkun.org/tikkundaily, TheReviewReview.net, San Jose's weekly, The Metro, and classism.org.

In 2013, she co-founded the Flash Fiction Forum, a reading series in San Jose.

Find out more about this artist:
https://www.facebook.com/Lita-Kurth-Writing-Workshops-201900896677647/

This story originally appeared in Dragonfly Press's DNA ezine. Reprinted with permission from www.dragonflypress-ca.com

Selected Poems
by Janice T

About this month's featured poet:

Janice T began to write poetry at the age of 11. While in the sixth grade, her class was given a writing assignment. What she wrote excited her teacher, who announced to his fellow teachers, "I have a poet in my class!"

Out of curiosity she went through her father's modest library in search of "poets." There she found a book titled, The Oxford Book of English Verse. The poems in this thick volume were written between 1250 and 1918, and included the works of the Lake District Poets. These poets became her teachers as she began to write her own poems.

Although her first piece was written in prose those many decades ago, (and, yes, she has dabbled in prose from time to time), Janice T almost always uses a Neo-Victorian voice.

Find out more about this artist:
http://janice-t.weebly.com/

A Rare Day

Sweet comfort breathes into the eaves
Imbuing all who dwell
Within this gentle hostelry
With peaceful ease as well.

A subtle breeze begins to tease
The window's wispy veil
While white waves breach the sunlit beach
And otters ride their swell.

Enveloping and nurturing
Composed to sooth and quell
This all too precious rarity
Consumes me with its spell.

The Nurture of Nature

Guard well this tender cradle.
In every aspect strive
To nurture as you're able
That you and all may thrive.

Be not in haste to gamble
This rich estate away
On promises of ample
Enrichments to be made.

No matter how beguiling
Scorn negligence and greed.
This is your bed and bounty
Your very life, indeed.

Guard well this tender cradle
For Nature, like a host,
Will set an ample table
For those who prize it most.

Pluviophile

I pull the curtains back
From windows clear and wide
In earnest, hopeful stance
To search the open sky
For merest wisp of cloud
In arcing ever blue
Until I burst aloud,
"The rain is long past due!"

Where is that swollen scent
When sea birds fill the air
And moisture not yet spent
Is lurking everywhere.
Why do they stay away,
This season's will defy?
Oh how I miss those days
When all the sky would cry.

When Sunlight Fails

When everywhere seems clouded gloom,
When disappointments press,
A famine of the heart presumes
That every joy is less

No matter gentle pleasantries
Nor comforting caress
Nor any offered remedy
To someone so depressed

Yet, ample joys there'll always be
To tug the sunken chest
Until what seemed sheer misery
Proves but a little test.

The Medicine We're Taking

Every spoonful is inclined
To dull the senses, bind the mind.
Beneath its candy coating find
The medicine we're taking.
Its every gram is time released
Extending our synthetic peace.
Though human problems seldom cease
There can be no mistaking
The power in this tiny pill
That quiets every thought and will
Unless one is immune or ill
Affected, thus forsaking.
Forsaken, then, as beasts unfit
Are those who do not swallow it
But heed a violent urge to spit
The medicine we're taking.

ARE YOU FAMILY YET?

If not, join the FSV Family today at the following URL: http://fictionsv.com/index.html

What are the benefits of being a family member?

I'm glad you asked.

1. Get FICTION Silicon Valley Monthly delivered direct to your eMail inbox every month (a $6.99 value - free because you are family).

2. Receive $1 worth of Bonus Bucks towards each paperback release of FICTION Silicon Valley Monthly.

There are even more benefits to becoming a Patreon Family Member: (http://tiny.cc/patreonfsv)

1. Receive a free eBook Upgrade to access additional formats of each FICTION Silicon Valley release in Kindle and EPUB. Get FICTION Silicon Valley Monthly for free in the format you love most.

2. Get up to $4 worth of Bonus Bucks towards each paperback release.

There are only benefits for becoming part of our family. You not only support great artists but you also receive amazing bonuses and upgrades to boot.

Join me now at FictionSV.com and be part of our family.